# The Dog that Saved the World (Cup)

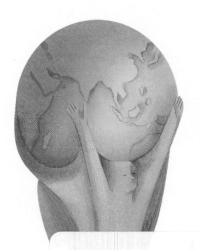

# The Dog that Saved the World (Cup)

Phil Earle

Illustrated by
Elisa Paganelli

Barrington Stoke

First published in 2021 in Great Britain by
Barrington Stoke Ltd
18 Walker Street, Edinburgh, EH3 7LP

www.barringtonstoke.co.uk

Text © 2021 Phil Earle
Illustrations © 2021 Elisa Paganelli

A CIP catalogue record for this book is available
from the British Library upon request

ISBN: 978-1-78112-968-5

Printed by Hussar Books, Poland

*To our Elsie, of course ...*

*... and to my friends at Barrington Stoke, who are by far the greatest team the world has ever seen*

I

Football is the best thing ever. Fact.

I mean, sleeping is great too, but when I dream, it's always about scoring goals. And I like eating – I'll scoff every scrap of food in my bowl, but only so I have loads of energy to chase a football all day.

Everything comes back to football in the end. Know what I mean?

I'm pretty good at it as well. I should be, given how much time I spend in the park dribbling, passing, practising my silky skills. I don't want to sound like a big head, but when people see me playing football, they stop and watch. Some of them even get their phones out and film me. They laugh and point and clap, which just makes me show off all my best tricks. There's nothing better than playing football in front of a crowd, and the bigger the crowd, the better. Some days in the park, we end up with so many people watching that it feels like we should be charging them.

"We'd make a fortune," Elsie always says. "Imagine how happy Dad would be if we went home with a hat full of cash?"

Elsie's right too. We haven't had much money lately, and it's caused Dad, and Elsie, a lot of worry.

Elsie has been my best friend ever since she was born. She's the person I always play football with. She's skilful, fast and has a properly powerful shot.

She's not as good as me, but that's OK. After all, there's a really good reason why I'm a better footballer. Two reasons, in fact: I've got four legs and Elsie only has two.

Anyway, football has always been our thing. It's what Elsie and I do, the thing that makes us best mates. And then recently, it became more than that.

Football took us on an adventure.  A BIG
ONE.

And this adventure changed Elsie's world,
and mine ...

## 2

There were three people in our team. No
substitutes, no big-money transfers in or out.
Just Elsie, Dad and me. It had been that way
for a long time, since Mum left when Elsie was
a baby. You could say I was the coach, and the
captain too, but Dad would have disagreed. He
liked to think he was the boss, the one who
decided the tactics on and off the pitch. But
when he tried to boss Elsie and me about, I just
talked over him. Loudly.

We lived in a flat down by the railway
tracks. It was small, but Elsie and I liked it cos
we got to share a room. Dad slept on the settee
in the living room.

"It's nearly 6.08, Pickles," Elsie said to me every night. "Ready for the roar?" And I pricked my ears up, my tongue lolling.

The 6.08 was a BIG train, one that thundered out of the city and all the way up to the north.

Elsie told me, "If you close your eyes and REALLY use your imagination, the noise of the train is like the roar of a football crowd. You know, when a winger goes on a run and everyone jumps to their feet!"

I have to admit, the roar didn't remind me of that at all. I didn't like it. The way the sound made the walls shake, knocking Elsie's medals off the old fruit crate she used as a trophy cabinet. But I made myself remember that Elsie is actually two years younger than me. If she could be brave and turn the noise of the train into something cool, then I could too.

So when the rumbling started, we'd always do the same thing. Elsie would jump to her feet and grab an empty toilet roll, pretending it was a microphone.

"Here comes Elsie," she would say, in her best commentator voice. "She picks the ball up inside her own half and beats one, two, three players as if they weren't even there."

As the train roared closer and louder, Elsie always jumped onto her bed, and I did the same, running in circles as if I was the winger. Or if I really wanted to make Elsie laugh, I'd dive on my back like I was one of the beaten defenders.

"This is a brilliant run," she'd yell, louder and louder to match the train's roar. And as the train whizzed past, Elsie would shout, "She sees the keeper off her line and shoots … GOOOOAAAAAL!"

And I'd bark "GOAL!" too, and Elsie and I would celebrate like we'd just won the cup.

It was the same every night, with the same response from Dad too.

"Will you two keep it down?" Dad always yelled from the doorway, holding the phone to his chest so the person at the other end couldn't hear. "I'm trying to close a deal here!"

Dad did a lot of that – "closing deals". I think it meant he was working. He sold things to people over the phone – that's what Elsie told me anyway. But it never seemed like anyone wanted what Dad was selling. It all sounded very confusing. To be honest, being a dog seemed a lot more fun. And simpler too.

But Dad always calmed down by the time we had dinner. And he always made it fun. Well, as fun as eating food that came in dented old cans could be.

"Dad," Elsie would say. "Why do we always have food from damaged cans? Is it because it's cheaper?"

"No, no, no!" Dad said. "Far from it. The dents make the food taste better. Makes it one of a kind."

I was never sure if Elsie believed him. Her face didn't look like she did.

Tuesday was always "soup night" and Wednesdays meant "bean feast", which was beans on toast (with cheese if it was a good week). Fridays were Elsie's favourite, as Dad called it "lucky-dip day". He would take the label off the can before opening it, then blindfold Elsie and make her guess the food inside just by sniffing. She was amazing at it. I thought I had a detective's nose, but it's nothing compared to Elsie's.

I always had dog biscuits by the way – dry, boring, tasteless biscuits. So I'd hide under Elsie's chair as she ate. She was a brilliantly messy eater, which meant I got to fill my belly AND keep the floor clean for Dad!

But what we both loved best was bedtime, as Dad always got us warm, no matter how rubbish dinner had been, or how cold it was in the flat that night. He'd heat a hot water bottle for Elsie, and one for me too. Then we'd snuggle down in her sleeping bag while Dad told us stories about a made-up footballer who took the world by storm despite being just sixteen years old.

Elsie always looked so happy as she listened to Dad. She would stroke me behind my ear until she fell asleep and whisper "goal" in her dreams as the late trains rumbled past.

I always stayed awake later than Elsie to make sure Dad was OK, but he never did anything very interesting. Mostly he sat at the table, warming his hands on a mug of tea, staring at lots of pieces of paper covered in red ink.

I've no idea what the letters said – I can't read, can I? But I think they were from someone called Bill, as Dad would say his name over and over again. Whoever Bill was, he couldn't have been very nice, as his letters always made Dad sigh and shake his head a lot. Sometimes, Dad even put his head on the table and made the sorts of noises I make when I lose my ball. When he did that, I always went over and licked his leg, which cheered Dad up no end.

Like I said, we were a team, the three of us.
And what do teams do, no matter what happens?

They stick together, that's what.

# 3

Wednesdays were the best days, because that was football training day for Elsie. She played for the Saints. Both boys and girls played for the team, but Elsie was the best. I trained her well: she was the fastest runner, the best tackler, and as for her shooting? Well, she was nearly as good as me. Nearly.

This particular Wednesday, Elsie and I were running ahead of Dad as we made our way to training. We couldn't wait to get there, and as we ran, Elsie couldn't stop talking about a VERY important footballing event that was coming up.

"Can you believe it, Pickles?" she said to me. "It's only a couple of months until the World Cup starts. I don't know about you, but I am WELL excited!"

I barked to let her know that I agreed.

"I mean, it's bonkers, isn't it?" Elsie said. "That the World Cup is taking place right here, in our country. Dad says it's decades since that happened. Do you think he might surprise us and take us to a match?"

I didn't think so, but I didn't want to burst Elsie's bubble. If Dad had got any tickets in the post, I would've seen them. Instead there had just been more and more letters from that chap called Bill.

"Imagine going to a match," Elsie went on. "All those thousands of people. If there was a goal, it'd be like five trains passing the flat at once!"

I loved seeing Elsie get so excited about the World Cup, and of course it was brilliant that football was "coming home", as Elsie said. But I knew that *I* wouldn't be going to a match any time soon. I'd watched hundreds of games on the telly and I'd never seen a dog in the crowd. I'd often thought about writing a letter of complaint, but then I'd remember that I couldn't read or write. And that I've got paws instead of fingers. It's not easy holding a pen in your teeth, I can tell you.

Anyway, we arrived at footie training, and Elsie started warming up with her friends. This was when I always started to feel a bit jealous. I might have been a great player, but Coach wouldn't let me take part in practice, and I had to stand on the touchline with Dad, on my lead.

After warm-up, the Saints normally moved on to drills, but today was different. Today, Coach called the players into a huddle.

"Exciting news, team!" Coach said. "You know the World Cup will be starting soon?"

Everyone nodded (including me).

"Well, we've been invited to enter a competition," Coach went on. "And the winners get to play a match during half time ... at THE WORLD CUP FINAL!!"

You can imagine how excited everyone was. I got so dizzy chasing my own tail that I got tangled up in my lead and fell over.

"All we have to do," Coach said, "is send in a video showing how skilful we are. The two teams who perform the best tricks will be chosen. So, what do you think?"

Well, of course nobody needed asking twice. Coach pulled out his phone and hit record, and everyone started showing off their best footballing tricks – lollipops, step-overs, flick-flacks.

It was all very impressive, but as I stood there and watched, I knew something the players didn't. Every team in the country would do the same thing. They needed something else, something different – something that would make the Saints stand out.

They needed me! I pulled so hard on my lead that the catch broke, allowing me to dash free and show the camera just what I was made of. I performed all my best tricks: around the world, switch scoop, rocket launcher. I was unstoppable. And after a minute or two, Elsie had a BRILLIANT idea.

"Let's put Pickles in a Saints shirt and film him!" she said. "We can make it look like he's our star player! We'll definitely win then."

That was fine by me – if it helped the team and, most importantly, it made Elsie happy. So I stood there as Elsie pulled a Saints top over my head and tied a knot in it to hold it in place.

The next five minutes were awesome.  There were gasps and lots of laughter as I bamboozled the team with my skills and scored goal after goal.  Then I ended by nutmegging Coach, much to his embarrassment.

*Did you get all that?* I wanted to ask Coach, but I gave him a lick to make him feel better instead. I knew that if he had filmed it, then the other teams might as well not even enter the competition.

The Saints, Elsie and I would be on our way to Wembley!

# 4

The next few weeks were very, very exciting.

There were adverts for the World Cup everywhere you looked. On the telly, in the newspapers, even on the sides of buses. There were huge photographs of the most famous footballers on the planet, all about to play in the biggest tournament ever!

Elsie and I didn't do a lot of sleeping, I can tell you. But we did do a lot of practising. If the Saints won the competition and were picked to play at the final, then we had to be on top form. So I worked Elsie hard, snapping at her heels if she started looking weak. "All right, all right, boy," Elsie said with a smile, looking tired.

But there was one person who looked even more pooped than Elsie did – Dad. It was strange, as I didn't see him training, not even for a minute, yet he had great big bags under his eyes. And he looked sad too – as sad as I'd felt the day I burst my favourite ball.

Fortunately, Elsie didn't notice Dad's tiredness. She was too gripped with World Cup fever. Plus, it's easy to forget sometimes that she's still only young. She doesn't see the world like I do. That's why I'm the boss, I suppose. So I kept a very close eye on Dad when Elsie was at school and he worked at the kitchen table.

The flat was always cold during the day. Dad turned the heating off and filled up both of our hot water bottles instead, shoving one down the back of his jumper and laying the other across his slippers.

I'd lie at Dad's feet, warming myself on the bottle, listening as he made his work calls.

"Good morning, madam, can I interest you in double glazing today—"

Most of the time the person hung up on him before Dad even finished the sentence, which always made me feel sad and more than a bit angry.

It upset Dad too. One day when it had happened ten times, he looked pale and tired. After another ten calls, I thought he might cry. Then he started looking at all of Bill's red letters again, which just made him look even worse.

I didn't stand around and watch him. Course not. I tried to cheer Dad up. Tempt him into a game of footie, rolling my ball to him with my nose.

"Not now, Pickles," Dad said. "I haven't got time to play. I haven't even got time to eat." Then he muttered, "I can't afford to eat anyway."

Now that really DID make me feel sad – so sad that I pushed my food bowl against his shin to show him that I was happy to share. But it didn't matter how many times I did it, Dad refused. In fact, in the end he got so cross that he shouted at me, which was most unlike him.

"For goodness sake, Pickles, STOP IT!" he yelled. "Can't you see it's all going wrong?"

And he buried his head in his hands and cried, then screwed every letter from Bill into a ball.

Now as you know, I LOVE a ball, but this was one game I didn't want to take part in.

Dad was sad, REALLY sad, and I was scared that there was nothing I could do to help.

# 5

Dad had dried his eyes by the time he and I reached the school gates later that afternoon. All Elsie saw was both of us smiling when she raced out of the door, kicking a ball as she went.

It was Wednesday, training day, so we headed down to the park.

As we arrived, all the Saints players stood surrounding Coach, and he was wearing the biggest of beaming smiles.

"Elsie," he said, "thank goodness you're here! That means I can tell you all the news."

Her team-mates beckoned her over, all with excited faces – the sort of face I'd have if every cat in the world had been thrown into prison.

"What?" Elsie yelled. "What is it?"

To be honest, I wanted to know too, and I turned to look at Dad to see if he had worked it out before us. But then his phone rang, and as he checked the screen his face turned whiter than an England kit.

*Who is it?* I wondered. *Don't answer the phone now, Dad. Coach is about to announce some big news!*

But Dad took the call, his face all lined and worried.

I didn't know which way to look. Should I focus on Elsie and hear her news, or Dad, to see what was going on there? It was a hard decision to make. Elsie might have been smaller than

Dad, but they were both my family.  I had to keep them both safe and happy.

In the end, I chose Elsie, but only because Coach was being so loud about it.

"You're never going to believe it," he said.  "I had to read the letter fifty times, then call the people to check it was true, but I've had the best news.  Not just the best, the GREATEST ..."

*Get on with it!* I thought, desperate to hear what Coach had to say.

"We won!  The competition ... to play at the World Cup final ... we only flipping well WON, DIDN'T WE?  We're on our way to WEMBLEY!"

And Coach leapt in the air like he'd just scored the winning goal in the ninetieth minute.  Of course this started all the others jumping too and chanting, "OLE!  OLE, OLE, OLE!"

Well, it would have been rude if I hadn't joined in, so I did, which got everyone laughing. Before I knew it, Coach had picked me up and was kissing me. I didn't like it very much, despite the number of faces I've licked in my life.

"It's all thanks to you, little Pickles," Coach yelled in my ear. "The judges of the competition thought you were the greatest!" He held me up in the air above his head like I was the World Cup trophy.

I felt so happy! It was a great day for the coach, a great day for the Saints and a wonderful day for my Elsie. But as I looked at Dad, all my happiness drained away. Because he was sad. He ended his phone call with a face full of sorrow and worry.

I squirmed out of Coach's arms, dashing to Dad and nuzzling him gently.

"Oh, Pickles," Dad said, his eyes full of tears again.

*What's wrong, Dad?* I wondered. *What's happened?*

But all he could say was, "What am I going to tell Elsie?"

And I could see him worrying about that all the way home.

# 6

Elsie was always excited after football training. She should've been tired, but instead she seemed to have even more energy. It was especially true that night after the big news from Coach. Questions flew out of Elsie's mouth at a million miles an hour.

"Do you think we'll get to meet the players?"

"Or hold the World Cup trophy?"

"Will we have to buy a new kit?"

"And I'll need new boots. Mine are a bit small."

I was excited for Elsie, of course I was. But with every question I could see Dad's mood getting worse and worse, especially when she asked about a new kit and boots. He started fidgeting and sighing, then he wasn't looking at Elsie as she spoke.

I didn't know why Dad was being like this, not really, but I thought he might feel better if I could calm Elsie down a bit. So I sat on her lap and licked her face to get her to shush. But it didn't work. It just made Elsie ask Dad questions about me too.

"Pickles will be allowed to come, won't he?"

"Cos if he can, then we should buy him a kit too, shouldn't we?"

"Can we, Dad? Can we? Pleeeease?"

Dad opened his mouth to speak, but no words came out.

He tried again. But there seemed to be a problem getting the message from his brain to his mouth.

"Your boots—" Dad said.

"It's OK, Dad," Elsie butted in. "You don't need to help me choose them. I know which ones I want. I'll show you." And she reached for Dad's old tablet, her fingers tapping the screen super-fast.

But as Elsie hit search, her brow creased with confusion. "That's funny," she said. "The internet isn't working. I'll try again." But every time she tried, the result was the same.

I racked my brain about whether the broken internet could be my fault. Sometimes I do a wee by accident when I get excited, but I didn't remember doing one on any important wires.

"Dad, what's wrong with the internet?" Elsie asked.

And this time Dad DID find the words, but I wished that he hadn't, as it wasn't good news.

"We're going to have to live without the internet for a while," he said, his face red with embarrassment.

"What? Why?" Elsie said.

Dad sat down on the sofa and called her over. "Listen, money has been tight for a while now. It's not been easy selling windows over the phone, and I only really get paid when people buy them. And ... well ... I haven't sold a single pane of glass in five weeks."

Elsie looked sad. I knew what she was thinking: how would she look at footie videos on YouTube without the internet? But she didn't say that. All she did was sit on Dad's knee and give him a hug. Fortunately, she left room for me to climb on too.

"Don't worry, Dad," Elsie said. "It's just a bad run. Strikers go weeks without scoring sometimes."

That should have cheered Dad up. It would normally, but not today. Instead his eyes started leaking tears again.

"Well, this striker has got concrete boots," Dad said.

"What do you mean?" Elsie asked.

"My performance has been so bad that my boss has fired me. I haven't got a job any more."

# 7

Dad was a good man. A very good man. He'd always worked hard, so when he lost his job, it changed everything.

At first, the weirdest thing was seeing Dad without his mobile all day. Elsie used to joke that a doctor had sewn his phone onto his ear, but now his mobile sat on the table most of the time, silent. Unused.

I could see how sad Dad was, but he didn't sulk or pity himself. Not that I'd let him. Whenever I saw Dad looking a bit down, I'd clamp my lead between my teeth and take it to him, telling him to get busy by walking me. He never said no. He'd smile and stroke me and then walk me, sometimes for hours, till my paws were sore.

As we walked, Dad would go into every shop we passed, tying me up outside. Once or twice I heard what he was saying to the person behind the till.

"I'm looking for work. Can you help? I'll do anything. Stack the shelves, mop the floor. I just need work."

But it seemed that Dad was always out of luck. It was the same answer in every shop he went into: a shake of the head, a simple response of, "No, sorry."

So we walked on. And on. Only stopping when it was time to pick up Elsie from school. Both of us pasted on our best smiles as she raced out of the doors, football in hand.

"Hello, trouble," Dad would say to her. "What do you want to do before dinner?"

Elsie would stand, hands on hips, frown on her face. "What do you think?" she would say. "The World Cup will be here before we know it. And if we're going to win that match, then I need to practise!"

Dad smiled like it was a surprise for her to say that, and we'd scoot to the park to pass and shoot and practise our skills until our bellies growled louder than I once did at a poodle who dared to steal my ball. (He never did it again.)

But I have to be honest and say that those days our bellies still growled AFTER dinner too.

"Is there any more, Dad?" Elsie asked one night. She'd just scraped every bit of bean juice off her plate with her finger.

"Of course. You can finish mine. I'm not hungry." Dad smiled, sliding his plate over. I'd noticed he'd started eating very slowly these days, and I knew he was doing it in case Elsie needed more.

But Elsie didn't realise. She was hungry, and as she demolished the food on his plate, Dad took a nervous sip of water before starting to speak.

"Listen, Elsie. I was thinking about this flat. And about how annoying the trains are, and how there's no space for us to play footie outside. I was thinking, maybe it's time for a change. What do you reckon?"

Elsie looked up from her beans and then around at the room. "But I like it here," she said. "This is our home. I've never lived anywhere else."

She had a point. We'd been here a long, long time – when Elsie's mum was here too.

"I know that," Dad sighed. He rubbed at his cheeks, which looked greyer and skinnier than they ever had. "But while I look for work, money is really tight, and we might need something a bit … smaller."

*Smaller?* I thought to myself. *Is he kidding? I can cross the living room in two seconds flat as it is, and he sleeps on the sofa every night!*

"I've found somewhere else for us to live," Dad said. "And it won't be for ever, I promise. It was difficult finding a place where we were allowed to bring Pickles …"

My ears pricked up. What did he mean? What was the problem with me?

"But in the end I found somewhere," Dad went on. "Well, the council did …" Dad put on his best smiley, positive face.

"Really?" said Elsie. "What's it like?"

"Well … it's different from here.  And it's not perfect.  But the good news is there's sort of a football pitch right outside."

Elsie's face lit up like a firework.  "Really?" she said, beaming.

"Yes.  Kind of.  And there'll be other kids to play with.  Plenty of them.  You can have a five-a-side game, easy."

Well, that calmed Elsie down a bit.  It was clear she didn't want to move, none of us did, but she seemed to think that it wasn't all bad news.

But me?  I wasn't so sure.  Dad's mouth was smiling, but his eyes weren't.  And that worried me.  A lot.

# 8

It's hard to be brave when everything you own is in bin bags around you. Even harder when you see that it doesn't add up to much. Aside from her football trophies and ball, Elsie didn't have much at all, and I only had my hot water bottle and food bowl, which I had licked extra clean, ready for the move. (It saved Dad having to waste washing-up liquid on it.)

I nuzzled into Elsie as she watched Dad pack up the kitchen, her eyes as wide as the dinner plates in his hands.

*Don't worry*, I wanted to tell her. *It'll be OK. Dad promised us, remember?* But I didn't think

it would make Elsie look less scared. She'd been like this for a week now as we edged closer to the big move. She had started waking up in the night, talking of bad dreams about the new flat.

"Shhh now," Dad had said to her. "It'll be different there, but it'll also be the same. It'll still be the three of us, and that's the important thing, isn't it?"

"But what if the other kids don't like me?  Or football?" Elsie fretted.  "Or what if you get a new job, then lose it?  Would we have to move again then too?"

I wanted to reassure her, but Dad did it for me.  He told Elsie that they couldn't worry about things that hadn't happened yet.  He didn't have a new job anyway, despite the miles we walked every day looking for one.  I had even searched down the back of the sofa for a job, but Dad stopped me, telling me not to pull the cushions onto the floor.

I knew Dad was worried, but he did a very good job of keeping his brave face on.  Today he even managed to surprise Elsie with a treat.

"You know how it's just a couple of weeks until the World Cup starts?" Dad said.

Elsie's big scared eyes were replaced by excited ones as she nodded wildly.

"Well, the trophy itself has already landed in this country," Dad went on. "And it's being taken around EVERY league football ground to be shown off. It's coming to the Tigers stadium in town next week!"

"You mean we can go and look at the trophy?" said Elsie. "Up close?"

Dad nodded. "You'll see it on the day of the final too of course, but only from a distance. But next week, when it comes to the Tigers stadium, you'll be so close you'll be able to see the names of the countries who've won it engraved on the bottom."

Well, that was it. It seemed like every bit of worry and fear that Elsie had been carrying about the new flat melted away. I saw her start to imagine standing there, right in front of the

World Cup trophy. Maybe she'd be allowed to lift it too?!

It made me feel so much better to see her being her normal happy self.

I just hoped she felt the same way when we moved.

# 9

Humans are odd sometimes. Well, actually they're odd most of the time, but the day we moved, Dad was especially odd. Maybe he was just tired, because none of us had really slept. Elsie had been having her bad dreams again.

"I thought we'd catch the bus to the new flat," Dad said. He spoke way too brightly, so I knew he was faking it. I looked at all the bin bags and rucksacks we had to carry and wished that we could get a taxi. I think Dad felt the same once we finally reached the bus stop. His face was the colour of a tomato and was pouring with sweat.

"I'll go back for the rest of our stuff when you're at school, Elsie," Dad said, but Elsie wasn't listening. Maybe she was thinking about getting up close to the World Cup trophy, but from the look on her face I didn't think so. I cheered her up by sitting on her lap for the whole of the bus journey.

"It's a long way from the old flat, isn't it, Dad?" Elsie said, after we'd travelled across the entire city. "We are going to be able to get to school, aren't we? And what about footie training?"

Dad put on his best "trying not to look worried or sad" face again (but he still wasn't very good at it).

"Think about it like this," he said. "If we have to spend more time on the bus, then you can do your homework while we travel."

Elsie didn't look too wild about that idea.

"Think about it," said Dad. "That means you'll have more time when you get home. More time to play footie."

"And training?" Elsie asked.

"You won't miss one session, I promise. We just won't go home before it starts. After school, we'll take our dinner to the park and wait for training to begin. You'll be first there. Coach will see how keen you are!"

Elsie thought about this. She could see it wasn't ALL bad.

"Listen, I know it's not ideal," said Dad. "But we have to try to turn it into an adventure. And it's exciting too, Els, getting to know a new part of town. New sights, new smells. Lots to discover."

Elsie nodded, looking back anxiously as the city centre faded into the distance behind us. She looked even more worried when the bus finally came to the end of its route and we got off beneath a huge flyover.

*I can't see that football pitch Dad promised us?* I thought, spinning around. All I could see was concrete and pylons and warehouses. The closest thing to a blade of grass were the weeds growing between the cracks in the paving slabs.

"It's just over here," Dad sighed. We trudged through a set of rusted iron gates, weighed down by our heavy bags.

Now, I didn't know what to expect, but our new home ... well, it was a bit of a shock.

It was BIG. And crumbly looking. It had been painted white once, but that must have been a long time ago. Bits of white paint clung onto the walls in places, but mostly it was now grey, or brown where the drainpipe had leaked. Then there was the graffiti. Some of it was good, REALLY good, but most of it was just words, and not good words either. The sort of words adults didn't want children saying. If my paws had been bigger, I would've covered Elsie's eyes to hide them from her. I would've covered her eyes to hide all of it, to be honest, as none of it looked good. None of it looked like home.

Dad must have been thinking the same thing, as he crouched down beside her, pulling her close.

"Listen, Els, I know it doesn't look like much, but I promise you, it won't be for ever. Just until I find another job."

"What is this place?" Elsie asked. "They don't look like flats."

"They aren't, my love. They were offices. For businesses. People used to work here."

"Might you find a job here then? It would be good if you didn't have to travel far to work."

Dad smiled weakly. "There's no work here now. The offices have been empty for years, and there are so many people looking for somewhere to live that the council have turned them into flats. And look! Look at all this space for you to have a kick about!"

Elsie and I looked.  There was space, it was true.  There was a whole empty car park, with traffic cones we could use for goals, but there was also a lot of broken glass.  More glass than there was weeds even.

"Is this the pitch you told me about, Dad?" she asked.

"It is."  He looked embarrassed, like he'd told a whopper of a lie and got caught.  "But look," Dad said.  "There are other kids too – kids you can play with, just like I said."

A group of children were giving each other rides across the car park on old chairs that must have come from the offices.  They were the ones that sit on wheels and spin really fast like you're on the waltzer at the fair.

The kids looked happy, and friendly too. They smiled as we passed and asked Elsie if she wanted a go.  I hoped she'd say yes, but she didn't.  She hid behind Dad instead.

"Maybe later, eh?" Dad told the kids. "Her name's Elsie. We're going to be living at number fifty-nine."

"Fifty-nine?" Elsie asked. "There are that many families living here?"

"More," Dad said, taking Elsie's hand as we passed a group of teenagers just inside the main doors. They were arguing and smoking and playing music on their phones. One of them flicked the end of his cigarette at me, which made all his friends laugh.

But we weren't laughing. We were ... scared. Especially Elsie.

# 10

I'll never forget Elsie's face when Dad opened
the door to the new flat for the first time.

It didn't fall, it collapsed. And I wasn't
surprised. It was tiny in there. Our old place by
the railway tracks was small, but it was cosy. The
walls there were painted in warm colours, and
there were curtains on the windows so we could
keep the outside world away if we wanted to.

But here? Well, the walls were a dirty
cream, all marked with nails and bits of broken
shelves. And there were whiteboards dotted
around the place too, covered in old messages
about jobs that needed doing.

"I thought we could paint our own pictures on there," Dad said, trying to be cheerful. "Or maybe we could draw a World Cup wall chart and record all the results on it. It'll be fun!"

Elsie nodded as she pushed aside the old tattered blinds by the window. I could see her reflection mixed in with the motorway and concrete and graffiti. But all I could focus on were her eyes, which were filling with tears fast. Too fast.

Dad tried to cheer Elsie up by taking her on a tour of the flat, but I knew that was a bad idea. It wasn't like there was much to see – pretty much everything was in one room. We had just one electric hob to cook on, plus a sink, and one tatty sofa that looked like it had been pulled out of a skip. Behind the sofa were two single mattresses laid on the floor.

"I'll put a curtain up around your bed as soon as I can," said Dad, stroking Elsie's hair. "It'll be cosy, like your own little den."

Elsie asked where the toilet was, then probably wished she hadn't when she saw it. It was in the corridor, and we had to share it with other people on our floor. It smelt funny, the

loo seat was cracked, and the handle needed
to be pulled a hundred times to make it flush
properly. It made me relieved that all I needed
for a toilet was a tree or patch of grass.

"It'll get better," Dad said, but he looked
as upset as Elsie did. "There are good things
around the corner, I know it."

But Dad couldn't tell Elsie what those good
things were just then, as there was a knock at
the door. We answered it and were greeted by
two smiling faces – an adult and a small boy.
The boy shoved a toilet roll into Dad's hand.

"Welcome gift," the man said. "My name is
Samir. And this is my son, Wasim. We're your
neighbours. We couldn't afford flowers, and
I bet the council didn't leave you a roll in the
bathroom."

Dad REALLY looked close to tears now. "That
is so, so kind of you," he said. "Thank you very
much. They certainly didn't leave a telly. Any

idea how we can watch the World Cup matches when they start?  We're BIG footie fans."

"That's an easy one to solve," the man replied.  "We have a screen.  It's not big or posh, but that makes it better, we think.  The more people we squeeze around the telly, the more it will feel like we are actually at the match!  You are welcome to join us for any game you like.  My wife would love it, I'm sure!"

Dad shook Samir's hand and thanked him, apologising for not having a gift he could offer in return.  Elsie stayed half hidden behind Dad.  Her face was no less worried, even after hearing how she could watch the matches.

*

But if she was scared now, it was nothing compared to how she felt on the first night in the office block.

It was SO NOISY. We could hear people shouting and arguing in the flats on both sides of us. The music from mobile phones seemed to bounce spookily off the walls outside, which led to more people shouting and arguing. Then we saw the lights of police cars zooming by and heard the sirens. But we couldn't work out if they were outside and coming to the flats, or just zooming along the motorway nearby.

The only good thing was that we weren't in a different room from Dad any more, so he could hold Elsie's hand. He even stroked my paw when I put it next to him.

He was a good man, Dad, and he needed to be, because we were scared. And that first night seemed to last for ever.

# 11

For the next few days, I kept a lookout for the good things that Dad said were around the corner. But at first there was no good news to be seen, apart from an ice cream van passing by that was never going to stop at our flats.

But finally, FINALLY, good news came in the shape of a football (as it so often does).

The World Cup started and Samir and his family welcomed us into their flat to watch the games, just as they'd promised. Their flat was the same as ours, except it had three extra mattresses on the floor. That was lucky, given how many people were there to watch the match.  There were loads of us, singing and chanting, and you should've heard the roar when our country scored.  I thought the roof was going to blow right off!

"Imagine if our country gets to the final?" Elsie said to Dad and me. "Imagine if I get to play on the same World Cup final pitch as all my heroes!"

"Maybe it'll happen if you wish hard enough," Dad said, which made Elsie smile wider than she had in ages.

Good times WERE round the corner, just as Dad had said, and the next day, another one came along.

"Today's the day!" Dad said, waking us up with a grin. "The day the World Cup trophy comes to town!" He was beaming like the old Dad, and his good mood rubbed off on us. "Rise and shine!" he boomed in his loudest, cheeriest voice.

"What time is it?" Elsie asked.

"Half past five. But if we don't want to wait in the queue all day, then we need to get to the Tigers stadium early. Don't you agree?"

We most certainly did, and we bounced out of bed and wolfed down our toast on the way to the bus stop. (I demanded the crusts, which are always the best bit.)

The bus ride seemed to fly by this time. It was so early there was hardly any traffic on the road, and we played a game of fantasy football, choosing our best team using players from all round the world. Dad was rubbish at it of course, and Elsie and I laughed at all his choices, which made him smile even more.

By the time we arrived at the Tigers stadium, we were in the best mood we'd been in for weeks. Away from the flyover and the concrete, it felt like the sun was beaming down on us. We jogged along to join the queue, pretending we were playing in the World Cup final (and we were winning, of course).

"Look," said Elsie as we turned the final corner, "it wasn't just us who wanted to get here early."

The queue was epic – so big you'd have thought the final itself was happening. But we didn't let it get us down. How could we? We were going to see the World Cup trophy!

Or so we thought. Because in fact Elsie's world was, very sadly, about to end.

# 12

"Why isn't the queue moving, Dad?" Elsie asked.

"Don't know," he replied, and craned his neck to look down to the front. "The doors were meant to open half an hour ago. I suppose it will be slow. Everyone will want to have their photo taken with the trophy."

But another half an hour passed, and the queue didn't move a centimetre. Not in the right direction anyway. What DID happen was that people started looking at their phones, gasping and throwing their hands to their faces, then leaving the queue. And it wasn't just one or two people.  Hundreds of people did exactly the same thing.

"What's going on, Dad?" Elsie asked.  "Look at your phone."

"I can't, Els, I don't have any data left for the month."  So instead, Dad and Elsie asked the man in front of us what was happening.  He turned and showed us the screen on his phone.

"WORLD CUP STOLEN!" Dad read out. "Armed robbers steal trophy on way to Tigers stadium.  Organisers furious – nation embarrassed beyond belief."

"That can't be true, can it?" Elsie asked.

"I'm afraid it is, my dear," the man replied. "The World Cup organisers have gone bonkers. They say they'll kick our team out of the tournament as punishment if the trophy isn't found.  Imagine that?  When they're already playing so well!"

Elsie looked to Dad. Was he going to tell the man he was wrong? But Dad didn't. Facts were facts, and so how could he argue?

"They can't kick our team out, can they, Dad?" Elsie exclaimed. "We could win the whole thing the way we're playing!"

"The organisers can do whatever they like," Dad said. "But we're not going to see the trophy today, Els. Let's just hope someone finds it fast, before they take it out on our team."

To say Elsie looked sad was an understatement. She'd been SO excited about seeing the trophy, nearly as excited as she was about appearing at the final. And now, to hear that our country might be kicked out of the tournament? Well, it was too much for her. Tears trickled from Elsie's eyes.

"Can we go and find it, Dad?" she begged. "The trophy can't have gone far, can it?"

"Oh, Els, it'll be long gone by now," Dad said. "The thieves will have got as far away from here as possible. Come on. There's no point standing around. We might as well go home."

Our faces dropped. Elsie and I didn't want to go back to the flat, not when we'd had such a great day planned. Broken glass and graffiti were nowhere near as exciting as seeing the most famous trophy in the world.

"Can we go to the park instead, Dad?" Elsie asked, with a bit of desperation in her voice. "I've got my ball."

"Let's do that," said Dad. He was hardly going to say no, was he? "Then we can get home in time for the evening match."

It sounded better than nothing, so we slowly trudged away from the Tigers stadium, not knowing that things were about to get even worse for Elsie.

# 13

No one slept well that night, despite Dad and I doing everything we could to cheer Elsie up.

We'd had an epic game of football in the park, just the three of us. It lasted so long that even I was tired! Then we found some sandwiches in a corner shop that were on sale. Boy, did they taste good. On the bus home, Dad entertained us with talk of the World Cup matches that had already taken place. He knew it would excite Elsie, just as watching tonight's game would when the bus finally, FINALLY, snaked its way across town to home.

But the tiredness didn't help her sleep, no matter how much footie Elsie had played or watched, not with all the noise outside. There were arguments and shouts, there were dustbins being kicked over and loud music blaring. No matter how nicely, or how angrily, Dad asked the neighbours to be quiet, the racket just wouldn't stop. By morning, none of us had slept at all.

"Let's cheer ourselves up with the sports news," yawned Dad, switching on the radio. "I bet the police have found the trophy by now."

But they hadn't. And that wasn't the worst of it.

"This news just in from the World Cup," said the newsreader. "The organisers have said they won't kick our country out of the tournament, despite the cup being stolen here ..."

Elsie started to run around the room like she'd just scored with a long-range volley, then the reporter interrupted her.

"Instead, they've said that if the trophy is not found or returned before the semi-finals, the whole tournament will be cancelled. Without a trophy to present, said the organisers, how can there possibly be a winner?"

And that was it. Everything seemed to go into slow motion.

Dad looked at Elsie. Elsie looked at Dad. And then tears started to pour from her eyes.

"They can't do that, Dad!" she yelled. "If they cancel the final, then we can't go to it. And if we can't go, then we can't play, and if we can't play, then what … what … what have we got left to look forward to?"

Dad looked horrified and crouched down in front of Elsie. "What do you mean, Els?"

"I mean I'm scared, Dad. I'm scared of living here. I'm scared about money. I'm scared about what we're going to eat and how we're even going to look after Pickles. I'm scared of everything, Dad. I just want to go back home. Can we do that? Please?"

Dad hugged her tightly. And I nuzzled in. But Dad didn't reply. He couldn't, because he was crying too. So I realised that it was up to me. I had to make everything all right. I made a promise to Elsie and Dad that whatever it took, I would do it. I'd make things OK again.

The only problem was, I didn't have a clue where to start.

# 14

Nobody was in a good mood for the next two days. It was like a big black cloud had settled over the whole country and refused to move. The only thing anyone could talk or think about at training or on the bus was the trophy being stolen and what would happen if it wasn't found.

People panicked too. The police panicked and called in the army to help search for the trophy, the army panicked and called in the navy, the navy panicked and called in the ... Well, you get the idea, don't you?

The only one not panicking or depressed in the whole entire country was me. I'd made a promise to my family, and I wasn't going to let them down.

Instead, I turned detective. I listened to every radio report, and every TV news bulletin. When Elsie walked me past the newspaper shop, I stopped and wouldn't move until I'd looked at the front page of every paper. I couldn't read them myself, but I knew if I refused to budge, Elsie would end up interested and read them out loud for me. I'm not a genius – it's just what us dogs do.

I was most interested in the photo of the person who was thought to have stolen the trophy.  Police had studied every bit of CCTV they could find and built an image of the thief.  His face was burnt into my memory, I made sure of it.  Every hair, every freckle, every mole.

When I closed my eyes, I could remember that his nose was a bit beaky, like a magpie's, that his left eye was narrower than his right, and that his ears were stupidly small, like they belonged on a child.  I became convinced, CONVINCED, that I'd spot him a mile off, as soon as he swaggered into view.

The only problem was, he didn't appear.  I looked and looked, and begged Elsie and Dad to walk me every minute of the day, but no matter how hard I stared at every person we passed, none of them were him.

In the end, even I began to panic.  The day of our country's semi-final arrived, and there was still no sign of the trophy.

I had to get Elsie out of bed and pulled her duvet off to tell her so.

"There's no point getting up," she sobbed. "Everything is awful. We're going to have to live here for ever."

Well, I wasn't having that. We didn't have time to give up. We had to search, so I dragged Elsie (and Dad) from their beds with my teeth. I didn't even give them a chance to eat breakfast, and ten minutes later we were on the prowl for the trophy. Or rather I was. Dad and Elsie were still wiping sleep out of their eyes.

An hour into our search, the unexpected happened: we found a lead, and it wasn't the one round my neck. We were in the park by the high road when we saw a man walking towards us carrying a tatty plastic bag. He was too far away for me to see his face clearly at first, but there was something about him that made the fur on my back itch, like I was suddenly covered in fleas. I shouted at him, which made Elsie pull my lead gently and tell me to be quiet. But as he came closer the feeling got stronger, and I shouted again and again. I wanted Dad and Elsie to look at him too. There was something about him that was somehow ... wrong.

I studied the man's face, but it wasn't easy. Maybe it was because of me shouting at him, but he kept his head down, so I couldn't make out the shape of his nose, and his ears were covered by a red woolly hat.

By the time he reached us, I was certain there was something dodgy about him, and there was only one thing I could do to prove it. I jumped on the man, fast and sudden, pulling my lead out of Elsie's hand as I went. The man fell to the ground with a thump, dropping his bag with a clang, and I followed him, heading straight for his hat with my teeth. I had to see his face and his ears clearly to be sure it was him.

"Pickles! NO!" shouted Elsie and Dad, but I wasn't listening. Within seconds I'd tossed the man's hat to the side and I saw his face properly for the first time. His hair was different from the image I'd seen in the newspapers. It had

been shaved close to his head, and he had a pitiful beard now too, but I also saw the same beaky nose and definitely the same tiny, child-like ears.

*IT'S HIM!* I realised. *The man who stole the World Cup!* And I started shouting as loudly as I could to anyone who'd listen.

But for some reason, Dad didn't seem to understand what I was trying to tell him. Instead he tried to help the man up while passing him his plastic bag. In the meantime, Elsie was now clinging on to my lead.

*What are you doing?* I wanted to yell. *Don't give him the bag. The World Cup trophy is probably inside!*

Well, at that point, the man knew I was on to him. He snatched the bag from Dad, pushed him to the floor and sprinted back in the direction that he came from.

I didn't need to be told what to do. I ran, dragging Elsie behind me. She shouted and shouted, but for once I didn't listen. We had to catch the thief, and we had to do it now!

The chase went on, past the duck pond and around the play park. I knew we would catch him. He might have been a master criminal, but he was a rubbish runner and, besides, Elsie and I had been in training for months.

But as the man neared the exit to the park, something odd happened. Instead of running straight to the gates, he edged really close to a large brambly bush, and I noticed that the bag was no longer in his hand. He'd dumped it! In the bush!

I veered left, not caring about the man any more, which took Elsie by surprise.

"Pickles! What ARE you doing?" she asked.

I was burrowing nose first into the thorns, not caring if they pricked at my skin. I could do this. I could keep my promise.

And then I saw the bag, deep, deep, deep inside the prickly jagged bush. But I wasn't going to give up now, and I pushed on, not stopping until the plastic was in my teeth. I pulled and pulled, feeling the bag rip on the thorns until it was nothing but shreds. Then it wasn't even the bag in my mouth any more, it was the most beautiful (and heaviest) trophy that I had ever seen.

Finally, I emerged from the bush, triumphant, with the sun glinting off the cup.

Elsie gasped. She couldn't believe her eyes. Now it all made sense to her.

But she wasn't the first to speak. A woman nearby was.

"Look!" she yelled. "Over there. That little girl and that dog. They've ... they've ... found the World Cup!"

# 15

The rest of the day was a whirlwind: a whirlwind which blew the big black cloud away.

Everywhere we looked, there was excitement: excitement and smiles.  And all of it was aimed at us.  I'd never been given so many treats in my life, and, to be honest, I had one serious tummy ache after a few hours of it.

Not that I cared.  It was worth it.  The treats were delicious, but more importantly, MOST importantly, Elsie was smiling again.  And that treat felt like it would last for ever.

Dad was smiling too, of course, but he also looked a bit overwhelmed.  He was OK when the police arrived to take the trophy. But when the TV cameras arrived, he got us out of there super-fast, like he wanted to protect us from too many people looking our way.

Within minutes we were on a bus. No one said much. I licked at my belly, hoping it would take the ache away, while Elsie stroked my back and smiled into the distance like she was watching a TV replay of her favourite goal.

Even the office block didn't seem as grimy as usual. The sun cheered it up, and the noisy neighbours were still asleep after last night's racket. So we made some noise of our own, first with a match in the car park and then when we crowded round the TV with our neighbours for the semi-final. We were noisy when we sang the national anthem, but you should have heard the roar when the final whistle blew. Our team had done it. We'd crushed the opposition. Our country was heading to Wembley for the final, and so were we!

But Dad didn't let us get too excited.  In fact, for the next couple of days he kind of kept us hidden away, even Elsie from school!  And every time the news came on the radio, he switched it off, but not before we heard some of what they were saying.

"The search continues for the dog who saved the World Cup," the announcer said.

Elsie beamed.  "They're looking for Pickles!"

"I know," said Dad, like he wasn't interested.

"So we should contact them!" Elsie said.

"I don't think so," said Dad.

"Why not?"

Dad thought about this long and hard.

"Because I'm embarrassed," he replied at last.  "Not of Pickles, and definitely not of you.

But I'm embarrassed that we have to live here and that I can't afford to give us more right now. And the second they find Pickles, they'll be here, knocking on our door, telling everyone about our life."

Elsie looked around her and nodded. "OK," she said.

"Is it really OK with you?" Dad asked.

"Yep. And I don't think Pickles minds either. He knows what he did, he got loads of treats, and he's going to the final, isn't he?"

"He is, my love," Dad said.

"Then that's enough," Elsie said. "Isn't it, boy?"

"Woof!" I agreed loudly.

And for once they seemed to understand.

# 16

The big day arrived.  The biggest day.  The World Cup final, where not only the two greatest teams would be playing but our Elsie as well.  And make no mistake, she was THE greatest (aside from me).

We walked along Wembley Way with the rest of the Saints team, and it felt like we were walking on air.  Crowds sang, horns blared and there were the colours of our country's flag wherever you looked.  It felt like nothing would stand in the way of our victory.

It was strange, but as we neared the stadium, people started pointing at me.  At first,

I ignored them, thinking it was because I was the only dog going to the match. But it seemed to happen more and more as we walked closer – more pointing, lots of smiling and people taking my photo. I smiled back, of course, despite not knowing why.

But the smiling stopped when we reached the entrance to the stadium.

"No DOGS," a security man said crossly, his belly so round it looked like he'd eaten a sofa.

"I'm sorry, what?" Elsie replied.

"I said, NO DOGS."

"But this is Pickles," Elsie stammered. I could see she wanted to tell the security man what I'd done but also knew Dad wouldn't want her to.

"I don't care if he's a cheese and pickle sandwich. Dogs are not allowed in the stadium."

Well, that was it, all hell broke loose. Coach got cross, Elsie started crying and the rest of the Saints team tried to tell the man what a good player Pickles was. But the security guy didn't care.

Not until a man tapped him on the shoulder and said, "Hey, pal. What's your problem with that dog? He should have the best seat in the house after what he did! He's famous."

"Oh yeah?" the security man said. "Who is he then? David Beckham in disguise?"

"I'll show you," said the man, and pulled a phone from his pocket. He tapped on the screen and then turned it around to show a photo of me with the World Cup trophy between my teeth. "This dog is a national hero. Without this dog, you wouldn't have a job today. Someone just sent this photo to the papers. This dog here ... he saved the world!"

I blushed beneath my fur and wanted to say, "And the World Cup. Don't forget that."

The security man seemed very doubtful, but he looked at the photo, then at me, and then he swept me up in his arms.

"You little beauty!" he cried, kissing me with his big slobbery lips.

*That's quite enough of that*, I thought, and wriggled out of his arms. I ran into the stadium, with Elsie, Dad and the Saints team all trotting along behind me.

# 17

The rest of the day was like a dream.  The best dream you ever had in your life.

By the time Elsie and her team ran onto the pitch at half time, our country was already a goal up.  But that goal was nothing compared to the hat-trick that Elsie scored: a header, a volley and a screamer from the edge of the box.  However, I'm embarrassed to say that the biggest cheer was for ... me.

In the last five minutes of the Saints' game, I was brought on as a substitute, and the announcer told the crowd on the loudspeaker, "Ladies and gentlemen, please give it up for today's guest of honour – the greatest four-legged player ever, and the reason we are all here today. It's the finder and saviour of the World Cup – Pickles the dog!"

The crowd went wild.

So I treated them to a proper show, performing every trick I knew. I tied the defenders of the opposing team in knots, leaving them relieved to hear the final whistle. We'd won!

We made our way back to our seats, but it took a while. Everyone wanted a photo and I couldn't let anyone down. By the time we'd finished, my paw was sore from high-fiving.

In fact, we missed the second goal of the match, scored just after half time. But we were back in our seats by the third goal. When the final whistle blew, leaving our country the winners, it was like being at the best party ever.

I can't explain to you how it felt to watch our captain lift the World Cup in front of all the fans. Because, actually, I didn't see him do it. I was too busy watching Elsie in Dad's arms, the twinkle in her eyes gleaming brighter than any trophy ever could.

It felt like the end of a story ... but also the start of another one.

Yes, I'd saved the world (cup), and yes, we'd be going back to the office block to sleep that night. But that was OK, as I had faith in Dad. I knew that it wouldn't be for ever.

But even if it was, we'd be all right.

Because Elsie, Dad and I are by far the greatest team the world has ever seen.


**THE END**

### The true stories that inspired
# The Dog that Saved the World (Cup)

We are surrounded by stories. Every second of our lives. They're out there, waiting for us to spot and write down. I find this so exciting – the fact that the next great story for me to tell might be hiding round the corner. But sometimes you don't even have to leave your house to find another great adventure to write about.

History is full of stories too.

It doesn't matter if something happened fifty or five hundred years ago, it can still become an exciting story.

I wrote this book because of TWO things that happened in real life. One took place over fifty years ago, and one much more recently.

Let's start with what happened in 1966.

That summer, the World Cup came to England for the first time. But four months before the tournament started, disaster struck! The World Cup itself (called the Jules Rimet Trophy) was on display at an exhibition in London when it was stolen. It was supposed to be guarded by security, but the guards were terrible, and when they went on a tea break, the trophy was swiped.

Everyone in the world was laughing at England. The police had no idea where to start looking for the trophy and a week later it STILL hadn't been found ... Until a dog named Pickles went out for a walk with his owner, Dave, in South London, around ten miles from where the trophy was stolen.

As the pair walked, Pickles suddenly became very excited, running in circles by a neighbour's car. Dave went to see what the dog was barking at and found a package wrapped in old newspaper and tied up with string. When he ripped the parcel open, the missing trophy was inside. Pickles had saved the world (cup)!

At that point, Pickles' life went crazy. He became a star. His photo appeared in every newspaper, he and Dave went on the television, and Pickles won medals and awards, including dog of the year. He even became a film star! Perhaps most impressively, Pickles was invited to a huge party with the England team when they won the World Cup. At the end of the party, the team went out to meet a gigantic crowd in the street, and the England captain, Bobby Moore, held Pickles in the air like he was the World Cup trophy itself.

I love this story. I love the fact that a simple family dog solved a crime that all the police officers in the country couldn't crack.  And I love the fact that it's about football, as footie is one of my favourite things in the world.

It probably would have been enough of a story to write down by itself, but then my son, Stanley, told me ANOTHER true story that I knew I had to write about too.

He had just finished a book by one of his favourite authors, Matt Oldfield, called *Unbelievable Football*, which is packed full of real-life stories about football.  The most interesting story in that book (according to Stanley) is about Fara Williams.

Fara is a really successful player, who has played for Everton, Reading, Liverpool and Arsenal.  She has also played a whopping 172 times for England, scoring 40 goals, including one on her debut.

She is without doubt a football legend.

What makes Fara's story even more incredible, though, is the fact that from the age of seventeen she was homeless for six years, sleeping in hostels and on friends' sofas. She was even homeless while she was playing for England, keeping it secret from a lot of her team-mates.

Can you imagine that? A homeless footballer playing for England?

When I think about footballers, I often picture them living in HUGE houses and driving sports cars. I never imagined that a footballer could have so little money that they end up homeless.

Fara's story really, REALLY moved me, just as it did Stanley. I think she's an incredible player and an incredible woman. Her bravery and strength are exactly the sorts of qualities that heroes in books have. I knew, the second Stanley told me Fara's story, that I wanted to write not just about Pickles the dog but also about a footballer who was homeless, like Fara was.

I changed Fara's name to Elsie (my daughter's name – she's an excellent player too) and made her much younger. I gave her a dog ... called Pickles, and together they save the World Cup while having the most excellent adventure along the way.

I hope this explains what I mean about being surrounded by stories. In life now, and in history too.

I promise you, stories are out there, waiting for you to spot and write down. So keep your eyes open. You might not find the stolen World Cup trophy ... but you might find an exciting story to tell instead.

Good luck!